Stories of GREAT PEOPLE

Martin Luther King, Jr.'s microphone

Gerry Bailey and Karen Foster

Illustrated by Leighton Noyes and Karen Radford

🌱 Crabtree Publishing Company

www.crabtreebooks.com

Mr. RUMMAGE has a stall piled high with interesting objects—and he has a great story to tell about each and every one of his treasures.

DIGBY PLATT is an antique collector. Every Saturday he picks up a bargain at Mr. Rummage's antique stall and loves listening to the story behind his new 'find'.

HANNAH PLATT is Digby's argumentative, older sister—and she doesn't believe a word that Mr. Rummage says!

Mr. CLUMPMUGGER has an amazing collection of ancient maps, dusty books, and old newspapers in his rare prints stall.

Crabtree Publishing Company

www.crabtreebooks.com

Other books in the series

Cleopatra's coin

Columbus's chart

Leonardo's palette

Armstrong's moon rock

The Wright Brothers' glider

Shakespeare's quill

Marco Polo's silk purse

Mother Teresa's alms bowl

Sitting Bull's tomahawk

Credits

AP/Empics: 33 top right
Bettmann/Corbis: 12 right; 13 bottom left; 13 top right; 15 top left; 15 center left; 17 center; 17 bottom; 18 bottom left; 18 top right; 18 bottom right; 25 center left; 27 top left; 28 top right; 30 center left; 30 top right; 32 bottom left
Dave Butow/Corbis SABA: 33 bottom
Johnny Crawford/Image Works/Topfoto: 30 bottom right
CSK archives: 10 top*
Dinodia/Topfoto: 21 top
David J. & Janice L. Frent Collection/Corbis: 25 bottom right; 30 bottom center
Geoff Greenberg/Image Works/Topfoto: 32 top right
Louise Gubb/Image Works/Topfoto: 14 bottom left
Matt Herron/Take Stock Photos: 26-27 bottom
Hulton/Corbis: 13 center left
Image Works/Topfoto: 9 top
The King Center, Atlanta: 9 center left; 10 bottom
Russell Lee/Corbis: 28 bottom right
Library of Congress, Washington DC: 14 top right; 26 left
Time Life/Getty images: 27 top right
Tom & Dee Ann McCarthy/Corbis: 35
National Archives, Washington DC: 13 bottom right; 29 bottom left
Roger-Viollet/Topfoto: 29 bottom center
Flip Schulke/Corbis: 32 bottom right
Joe Sohm/Image Works/Topfoto: 9 center right
Time/Life/Getty Images: 25 right
Topfoto: 22 bottom left; 22 top right; 29 top right

Picture research: Diana Morris info@picture-research.co.uk

Library and Archives Canada Cataloguing in Publication

Bailey, Gerry
  Martin Luther King Jr.'s microphone / Gerry Bailey and Karen Foster ; illustrated by Leighton Noyes and Karen Radford.

(Stories of great people)
Includes index.
ISBN 978-0-7787-3689-9 (bound).--ISBN 978-0-7787-3711-7 (pbk.)

  1. King, Martin Luther--Juvenile fiction. 2. African Americans--Biography--Juvenile fiction. 3. Baptists--United States--Clergy--Biography--Juvenile fiction. I. Foster, Karen, 1959- II. Noyes, Leighton III. Radford, Karen IV. Title. V. Series.

PZ7.B15Mar 2008   j823'.92   C2007-907625-4

Library of Congress Cataloging-in-Publication Data

Bailey, Gerry.
 Martin Luther King Jr.'s microphone / Gerry Bailey and Karen Foster ; illustrated by Leighton Noyes and Karen Radford.
  p. cm. -- (Stories of great people)
 Includes index.
 ISBN-13: 978-0-7787-3689-9 (rlb)
 ISBN-10: 0-7787-3689-X (rlb)
 ISBN-13: 978-0-7787-3711-7 (pb)
 ISBN-10: 0-7787-3711-X (pb)
 1. King, Martin Luther, Jr., 1929-1968--Juvenile literature. 2. African Americans--Biography--Juvenile literature. 3. Civil rights workers--United States--Biography--Juvenile literature. 4. Baptists--United States--Clergy--Biography--Juvenile literature. 5. African Americans--Civil rights--History--20th century--Juvenile literature. 6. Civil rights movements--United States--History--20th century--Juvenile literature. I. Foster, Karen. II. Noyes, Leighton, ill. III. Radford, Karen, ill. IV. Title.
 E185.97.K5B335 2008
 323.092--dc22
 [B]
          2007051260

Crabtree Publishing Company

www.crabtreebooks.com 1-800-387-7650

Published in Canada
Crabtree Publishing
616 Welland Ave.
St. Catharines, Ontario
L2M 5V6

Published in the United States
Crabtree Publishing
PMB16A
350 Fifth Ave., Suite 3308
New York, NY 10118

Published by CRABTREE PUBLISHING COMPANY
Copyright © 2008 Diverta Ltd.

Martin Luther King, Jr.'s Microphone

Table of Contents

"Every Saturday morning, Knicknack Market comes to life. The street vendors are there almost before the sun is up. And by the time you and I are out of bed, the stalls are built, the boxes are opened and all the goods are carefully laid out on display.

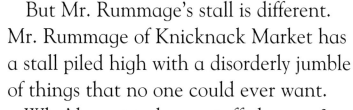

Objects are piled high. Some are laid out on velvet: precious necklaces and jeweled swords. Others stand upright at the back: large, framed pictures of very important people, lamps made from tasseled satin, and old-fashioned cash registers, the kind that jingle when the drawers are opened. And then there are things that stay in their boxes all day, waiting for the right customer to come along: war medals laid out in straight lines, watches on leather straps, and utensils in polished silver for all those special occasions.

But Mr. Rummage's stall is different. Mr. Rummage of Knicknack Market has a stall piled high with a disorderly jumble of things that no one could ever want.

Who'd want to buy a stuffed mouse? Or a broken umbrella? Or a pair of false teeth?

Mr. Rummage has them all. And, as you can imagine, they don't cost a lot!

Rummage's
Antiques

"Wow, I like this," said Hannah, picking up a battered microphone. "Ladies and gentlemen," she yelled into it, "I present to you the amazingly talented popstar Hannah…"

"Oh no!" sighed Digby, "what's she found now?"

"I think I'd better have that back, young lady," said Mr. Rummage, smiling. "It's an important microphone—and definitely not for budding stars."

"It looks kind of old fashioned, don't you think?" said Digby as Hannah handed the object back to Mr. Rummage.

"That's because it's an old model," said Mr. Rummage. "It dates back to the 1960s and was used by a great American, Martin Luther King, Jr. to make a very special speech."

"Very special!," said a voice from behind them. "Martin Luther King, Jr. was a great speaker. And I have something rather special of his to show you, too."

"Hi Mr. Clumpmugger," said Hannah. "I don't suppose you've got a video of one of his speeches, do you?"

"No, but I've got the next best thing," he smiled. "A book of his sermons—which I'll show you as soon as Mr. Rummage begins his story, as I'm sure he will."

"I can't wait," said Digby excitedly. "Martin Luther King, Jr. sounds really cool."

✝ MARTIN LUTHER KING, JR. ✝

Martin Luther King, Jr. was born on January 15, 1929, in Atlanta, Georgia. He was named after the famous Protestant reformer Martin Luther, as was his father, the reverend Martin Luther King, Sr.

Young Martin Luther King, Jr. was brought up with his brothers and sister near Ebenezer Baptist Church, where his father was a preacher.

Martin Luther King, Jr. dedicated his life to fighting for the rights of African Americans. He is remembered for his work as a church minister, his powerful speeches, and his determination to make changes in the United States.

Let's find out more...

Martin Luther King, Jr. is sitting in the front row, on the right.

School days

Life was difficult for young African Americans, especially in the southern states. As Martin Luther King, Jr. grew up he discovered that black people and white people were treated differently. For example, African Americans weren't allowed to drink from the same water fountains or use the same restrooms as white people. When Martin Luther King, Jr. went to school, he had to attend one for black children. His white friends went to a different one. Sadly, he was never allowed to play with his white friends again. But Martin Luther King, Jr. was comforted by his strong religious beliefs. He soon decided that he would become a church minister like his father and grandfather.

Martin Luther's family

In college, Martin Luther King, Jr. gained a PhD degree and became Dr. King. He also met Coretta Scott who became his wife. They went on to have four children: Yolanda, Martin Luther III, Dexter, and Bernice. Dr. King accepted the job of pastor at the Dexter Avenue Baptist Church in Montgomery, Alabama.

"You mean he was a preacher?" asked Digby.

"Yes, he was a minister of the Baptist church," said Mr. Rummage. "In fact, his father was also a minister and he had a big influence on Martin Luther King, Jr."

"Sounds like his dad wanted him to be a goody-goody," said Hannah.

"Not at all. Reverend King taught his children to treat everyone with respect. At the same time, he did his best to encourage the white and black people living in his parish to live together peacefully and happily."

"African Americans were descended from **slaves**, weren't they Mr. Rummage?" asked Digby. "The whole thing began after Christopher Columbus landed in the Americas. I remember that from one of your other stories."

"Well, you're kind of right, Digby. Black Africans were carried in ships to America to work on farms called **plantations**. Selling people as slaves was a terrible trade. Eventually, slavery was outlawed, but some white people still saw African Americans as inferior and thought they shouldn't have the same rights as white people. That's the barrier Martin Luther King, Jr.'s father was trying to break down."

"It sounds as though he couldn't have had much luck," said Hannah.

"And you're right. When young Martin Luther King, Jr. grew up, he noticed that it was a difficult world for African Americans."

"Did he have any white friends?" asked Digby.

"Yes, his best friend was a white boy. But they had to go to different schools, and after the first day of school they were never allowed to play together again."

"It must have been awful for Martin Luther not being able to play with his friends and being sent to a different school," said Hannah.

"It was bad for African Americans all over the United States," agreed Mr. Rummage. "There were a lot of problems that had to be solved if the country was to be a real **democracy** where everyone was treated the same."

"What kind of problems?" asked Digby.

"Well, there was something called segregation—racial laws that kept Martin Luther King, Jr. and his friends apart," said Mr. Rummage. "And then there were race riots, problems caused by African American workers leaving the South to find jobs in cities, and racial hatred spread by violent groups of white people."

Segregation

Segregation was the result of laws that kept black people apart from white people. African Americans were not given the same rights. And there was very little they could do about it because the law was controlled by white Americans.

African Americans were kept apart from white Americans.

Bad laws

Segregation was humiliating. African Americans had to sit at the back of buses and in separate railway cars. They couldn't eat in white-only restaurants, or compete in sporting events with whites. They weren't allowed to hold important public positions and they couldn't get the same jobs as white people. In many ways African Americans were being treated as second-class citizens. Something had to change!

SOUTH NORTH

When slavery ended, many African Americans headed north to find jobs. The North and the South of the United States were like two different worlds. The South was an old-fashioned farming area, while the North was a booming industrial zone with fast-growing cities. Many northerners were worried that African American workers would bring the problems of the South with them if they moved to the North.

The walls of this little boy's house are covered with newspaper to keep out the cold.

An African American family heads north to start a new life in the city.

The children of African American workers went to poorly equipped schools on plantation estates.

Most African American families came from the plantation regions of the South, where their parents had been taken as slaves.

"What a terrible way to treat people," said Hannah angrily.

"What happened isn't easy to understand, Hannah," said Mr. Rummage, "especially when you look at the lives of real people."

"Yes," said Digby, "I suppose you really feel it when it's your own family that's been treated badly."

"That's right," continued Mr. Rummage, "and what happened to some people made a lot of others pay attention. It helped change come about. Take the poor boy Emmet Till, for example."

"Was he a friend of Martin Luther King, Jr.?" asked Digby.

"No," answered Mr. Rummage, "but his sad story influenced Martin Luther King, Jr. very much.

"What happened?" asked Hannah, in a worried voice.

"Emmet went on a trip to a place called Money, Mississippi. His mother warned him how to behave there, as whites and blacks didn't get on as well as they did in his hometown of Chicago. Unfortunately, he didn't listen to her advice. Emmet was brutally murdered the same year Martin Luther King, Jr.'s first child was born."

Ku Klux Klan

Some people wanted to scare African Americans into not fighting for equal rights. They formed organizations dedicated to keeping white people in control. The worst of these groups was the **Ku Klux Klan**. Wearing white cloaks with pointed hoods to keep their identity secret, their aim was to badly frighten anyone who wasn't white. From 1868 to 1871, the Klan lynched over 400 African Americans—mostly in the deep South.

The burning cross was a fearful symbol of the Ku Klux Klan.

EMMET TILL

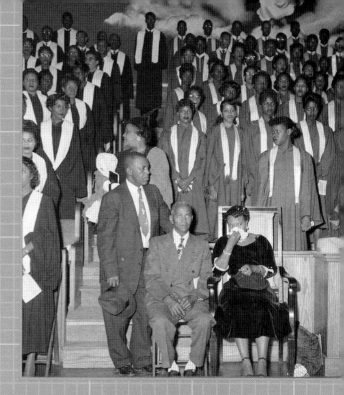

A few days after arriving in Mississippi, Emmet Till and his cousin Curtis went into town to buy candy. Outside the store, Emmet showed some local boys pictures of his white friends in Chicago. They dared him to talk to Carolyn Bryant, the candy store owner, who was white. He did and apparently left the store saying "Bye, baby"—or perhaps he whistled at her. We don't know for sure.

Word spread quickly. Soon Roy Bryant, Carolyn's husband, and his brother turned up at Emmets house. They took him away with them and threatened to kill his Uncle Mose if he said anything. Emmet had been hunted down because he dared to speak to a white woman.

Later, Emmet was found in the Tallahatchie River, weighed down by a cotton gin fan and with his face mutilated. The Bryants were arrested, but the white jury didn't convict them. So the killers got away with their crime.

But Emmet's mother was determined that the whole world should see what had been done to her son. She held an open casket funeral in Chicago. When the terrible story came out in the papers, both blacks and whites were shocked by it. **Racism** couldn't be ignored any more.

Thousands came to pay their respects at Emmet's funeral.

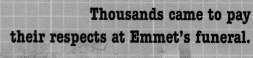

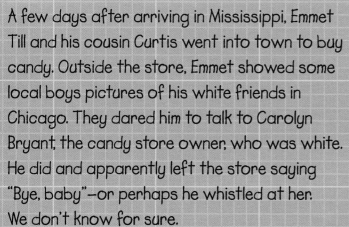

"It must have been difficult for African Americans not to get angry," said Digby.

"In a way, Digby, that's what some white people wanted—so they'd have even more excuses to behave badly," said Mr. Rummage. "And that's why Martin Luther King, Jr. was so determined to have peaceful protests."

"How did they protest peacefully?" asked Hannah.

"Well, one way was to ignore the rule of segregation on buses and sit where they wanted."

"Did Dr. King refuse to sit at the back of a bus?" asked Digby.

"No, but a brave lady called Rosa Parks did. She lived in Montgomery, Alabama, where Dr. King was pastor. In December of 1955, she refused to give up her seat in the bus she was riding so that a white passenger could have it. She was arrested."

"Arrested!" yelled Hannah. "For not giving up her bus seat to a white person?"

"Yes, and when Dr. King heard about it, he held a meeting at his church and told a huge crowd that the only way to protest was to **boycott** the buses by refusing to travel on them."

"Wow, how long did they do that for?" asked Digby.

"Over a year," said Mr. Rummage. "And it wasn't easy. Black people were threatened and Dr. King's house was bombed. Luckily his wife and baby daughter escaped unhurt. But it worked. Just a year later, Dr. King and another minister were able to share the front seat of a bus in Montgomery."

"Yeaaaah!" cheered the children.

ROSA PARKS

Rosa Parks may have been too tired to stand. Or she may just have been fed up with having to give up her seat on the bus if a white person wanted it. So on December 1, 1955, she refused to give up her seat when the driver yelled at her to move. She didn't argue or fuss. She just sat there bravely, knowing she could be putting her life at risk. Eventually the police were called and Rosa was arrested for her "crime."

A new leader

Because Rosa was well known in the black community, people took notice of the incident. The black leaders of Montgomery decided to organize a protest and made the young and popular minister, Martin Luther King, Jr. its president. A month later, after a stirring meeting led by Dr. King, a bus boycott began.

DO NOT RIDE A BUS TODAY

Bus boycott

At first, the Montgomery Bus Company thought everyone would soon be back on public transit. After all, most protesters were poor with large families and couldn't afford to miss work. They were wrong. As the weeks went by, the company lost money and ticket prices went up. Matters kept getting worse. Eventually, the protesters won and the United States Supreme Court was forced to decide that segregation on buses was illegal.

Boycotters chose to walk, share cars, or pedal bicycles to get to work, instead of boarding a bus.

LITTLE ROCK

Most American schools tried to **integrate**, or bring together, black and white students under the same roof. But in the South, some school boards refused. At Little Rock, Arkansas's Central High School, the National Guard were called in to block African Americans from entering. But the president sent federal troops to accompany them to their classes and to act as their personal bodyguards.

School bullies

Even though they had protection, the nine black students were insulted by white students. Their lockers were trashed and burning paper thrown at them in the restrooms. One gang threw a lighted stick of dynamite at a girl called Melba Pattillo, stabbed her, and threw acid in her eyes. And then the troops left and the African American students had to fend for themselves.

Graduation

Eventually, the first black student graduated from Central High School. What had happened at Little Rock had been a lesson for everyone. It showed that black students could win out in the end, if they stood their ground!

"I boycotted the candy store once," said Hannah. "They refused to stock my favorite chocolate bar…"

"Big deal!" said Digby, rolling his eyes. "So what did Dr. King do next, Mr. Rummage?"

"Well, after the bus boycott, his life was in danger. Imagine finding an unexploded bomb on your front porch or someone trying to stab you in a bookstore!"

"But why did people want to kill him?" asked Digby, scratching his head.

"Some people just didn't want a truly democratic United States," Mr. Rummage went on, "and they wanted to get rid of him. That included African Americans, you know. Tensions were running high in those days and people were often scared."

"Couldn't the government do something—like make them all live together without segregation?" asked Hannah.

"Well, the Supreme Court did rule that segregation was illegal. But many schools, especially in the South, kept up the old ways. And that led to situations like the Little Rock, Arkansas, case."

"I've heard of that," said Digby. "Didn't the army have to take kids to school?"

"Yes," answered Mr. Rummage, "the president sent troops to protect African American students going to Little Rock's Central High School. It was the only way. That's the sort of hateful prejudice Dr. King had to deal with."

"He must have been a very brave man," said Hannah admiringly.

"Dr. King was brave all right. He got a lot of inspiration from the Indian leader, Mahatma Gandhi."

"Wasn't he the man who helped get freedom for India?" asked Hannah.

"That's right, and Martin Luther King, Jr. went to India to meet the great man himself," continued Mr. Rummage. "While he was there, he studied "Satyagraha.""

"Who's that?" asked Digby.

Mr. Rummage laughed, "Not 'who,' but 'what,' you mean! It's Gandhi's word for peaceful protest. It means persuading people to do things without using physical violence."

"Did Mr. Gandhi get attacked as well?" asked Digby.

"Yes, he was arrested, thrown into jail, and abused. In a sense, Dr. King's life was a kind of copy of Mahatma Gandhi's," said Mr. Rummage. "In fact, when he returned to America, Dr. King took some of Gandhi's ideas back with him."

"I think you could do with a few of Gandhi's ideas," smirked Digby, poking Hannah in the ribs.

"Hey—no violence!" yelled Hannah.

"Come along you two," laughed Mr. Rummage, "stop arguing…we've got to get on with the story."

GANDHI

Born in 1869, Mohandas Karamchand Gandhi was a shy boy, but that didn't stop him from traveling on his own to London to study law. He earned his law degree there, and after practicing in India, went to South Africa to work. There he saw how badly minority peoples were treated. He often defended them in court, and during this time developed his idea of protesting without violence. He was sent to prison three times before returning to India.

Civil disobedience

Gandhi believed that if a law was unjust it should be changed or ended. One way of highlighting an unjust law was to deliberately break it. This was called **civil disobedience**. But civil disobedience had to be carried out without violence. The people involved had to be prepared to accept the consequences of their actions, even if it meant going to jail.

Success at last

In the end, Gandhi and his followers succeeded in drawing the world's attention to the injustice of British rule in India. They also showed that civil disobedience is a very powerful weapon when used properly. India became an independent country in 1947.

UNREST IN ALABAMA

The "Bull"

Theophilus Eugene "Bull" Connor was a scary individual—especially if you were African American. He was the police chief in Birmingham, Alabama, and he was against the idea of equal rights for African Americans. In fact, his ambition was to make sure that integration never took place in his city. But in April of 1963 he made a big mistake. Connor ordered his officers to use snarling dogs and powerful water hoses to break up a peaceful **civil rights** march led by Dr. King. His cruel actions were broadcast to the world and he became a symbol of extreme racism. People were disgusted by what they saw. Connor lost his job and instead of stopping the civil rights movement, he actually helped it grow.

Sit-in in progress

Later that month, Martin Luther King, Jr. joined civil rights protesters in a sit-in at a restaurant in Birmingham that segregated African Americans and whites. In these peaceful protests, people sat down and refused to budge until they were served food. King was arrested and the civil rights movement received even more publicity—just what it needed!

"So Martin Luther King, Jr. was prepared to go to jail for what he believed in," said Digby. "That must have been difficult, especially for his kids,"

"He had to do it. He had to show that he was prepared to suffer so others would follow him," said Mr. Rummage. "In 1960, he was arrested for "trespassing" in a white-only restaurant in downtown Atlanta. Although the charges were dropped soon after."

"Good," said Hannah defiantly. "I'm glad he was freed."

"But he wasn't," said Mr. Rummage. "He'd previously been let off for driving without a license. So the judge reinstated that charge and sentenced him to four months hard labor instead."

"That was a dirty trick," said Digby. "They were just making things up in order to arrest the protesters."

"Sort of. But Dr. King continued his efforts, while civil rights protesters rode segregated buses, staged sit-ins, and got arrested by racists like the police commissioner Eugene 'Bull' Connor, who set dogs on peaceful marchers."

"The civil rights movement was really beginning to take off," said Digby.

"Yes," said Mr. Rummage, "and King was such an inspirational speaker that thousands came to hear him."

"Did he learn that preaching from the pulpit?" asked Hannah.

"He probably did. He certainly knew how to work a crowd," said Mr. Rummage.

Hannah took the microphone and looked out over the market. "I have a dream," she began, speaking into the mike. "Isn't that one of his speeches?"

"It certainly is," said Mr. Clumpmugger, holding up a black notebook in his hand, "and some of the words of that speech are written right here."

"Is that the book of sermons you were talking about?" asked Digby.

"It sure is," replied Mr. Clumpmugger as the children came around to look at it.

"Even his writing would make you want to follow him," said Hannah, admiringly. "How much will you charge for it?"

Mr. Clumpmugger smiled, "It's not for sale, Hannah. Dr. King's a hero of mine—and this is a priceless souvenir."

THE 16TH STREET BAPTIST CHURCH TRAGEDY

For many months, the homes and churches of African Americans in Birmingham, Alabama, were bombed with dynamite. The most tragic of these incidents happened when four innocent black girls were killed in the basement of their church one Sunday in 1963. The girls were wearing their Sunday best as they prepared their lessons for the 11 o'clock service when the bomb exploded next to them. Dr. King gave a speech at their funeral—it made the international headlines.

Nobel Peace Prize

The Nobel Peace Prize is awarded each year to the person who has done the most to make the world a more peaceful place. Martin Luther King, Jr. won the prize in 1964 along with $54,000. He decided to divide the prize money between different civil rights organizations. In 1963, Time magazine voted him their "Man of the Year." Dr. King had become world famous.

FROM SELMA TO MONTGOMERY

Ambushed!

Dr. King organized a march in Alabama from Selma to Montgomery, the state capital. He planned to ask Governor George Wallace to protect African Americans who wanted to register to vote. But the march only got as far as the *Edmund Pettus Bridge*. On the bridge, the marchers were met by Sheriff Clark's posse and state troopers with gas masks on. The marchers were ordered to go back, but before they could do anything the troops charged them with tear gas, clubs, whips, and rubber hoses wound with barbed wire.

Many, many people were hurt. Dr. King wasn't there because he'd received death threats. But what the Sheriff hadn't bargained for was that the attack would be shown on television. The nation was horrified.

March to victory

A few days after the horrors of the first march, President Lyndon Johnson sent troops, marshals, and FBI agents to offer protection to the protesters. On March 25, Dr. King led 25,000 people on a five-day trek from Selma to Montgomery. People marched by day and camped in fields and on the roadside by night. A petition was handed to Governor Wallace, and Dr King and others addressed the large crowd. It was a huge victory.

"It must have been fun to march with Martin Luther," said Digby, beaming.

"Yes, but it was dangerous, too," said Mr. Rummage. "For example, in 1964 students campaigned to get more African Americans registered to vote."

"Why? Didn't they want to vote?" asked Hannah.

"Oh they wanted to vote, all right," replied Mr. Rummage. "But white registrars used every trick in the book to turn down their applications. If someone forgot to cross a 't,' the application would be thrown out."

"So they protested, I suppose," said Digby.

"Right. Some marched bravely to the courthouse to register, but they were stopped and arrested by Sheriff Jim Clark and his men. Clark was as bad as Bull Connor. Dr. King was asked to help. But more marches meant more arrests, including Dr. King's."

"Did all of this happen just in the southern states?' asked Digby.

"No," said Mr. Rummage, "there was trouble in the north, too. But one of the worst disturbances took place in a poor part of the city of Los Angeles called Watts."

"I thought laws like the Civil Rights Act were supposed to stop bad treatment," said Hannah.

"They were, but some states used all kinds of ways to get around the new federal laws."

"But didn't they have to do as they were told?" asked Digby, looking confused.

"No, they're very independent," answered Mr. Rummage. "That's the way the United States works. Individual states can make their own laws, and they may be very different from state to state."

"Doesn't sound very 'united' to me," grumbled Hannah.

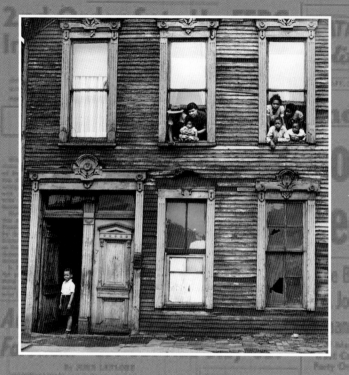

Dr. King and poverty

Martin Luther King, Jr. came to believe that poverty and unemployment were the main cause of unrest in America. But he wasn't worried about just African Americans. Poverty, he said, affected whites, Hispanics, and Asians just as badly.

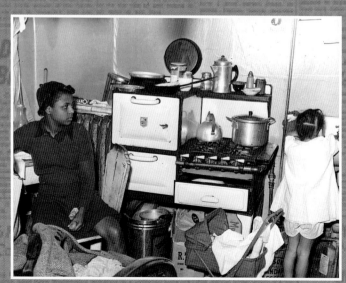

WATTS RIOTS

The state of California didn't want to provide African Americans with better housing, and this caused feelings of despair and outrage in the inner cities. It wouldn't have taken much to spark a riot. And that's just what happened on August 11, 1965, when a white motorcycle policeman pulled over an African-American driver, Marquette Frye. Apparently, someone said he'd been drinking. A crowd gathered around as Frye and his brother were questioned. When a scuffle broke out, the police used batons to beat them, which angered the crowd. Shortly after the police left, the rioting began.

Soon, Watts was in flames. Rioting spread throughout the area and snipers manned rooftops, shooting at the police. Fire trucks and ambulances were called to stop the violence, while 20,000 steel-helmeted national guardsmen went on patrol. After six days of rioting, 34 people, including children, had been killed. Over 1,100 had been wounded and 4,000 arrested. Watts was named a disaster area by the president, who said that African Americans had used the very methods they had spoken out against. But many thought that police brutality was the real culprit. Nevertheless, little was done to rebuild what had been destroyed during the riots.

"Despite the rioting, Dr. King continued his work through the mid-sixties," said Mr. Rummage. "Then in 1968, he was asked to help the black garbage collectors in Memphis, Tennessee. They were on strike because the city officials refused to recognize their mostly-black union. On March 18, Dr. King spoke to a rally of 15,000 strikers. Then, ten days later he led a march. But, to his horror it turned violent."

"Dr. King must have been really upset," said Hannah.

"He was," continued Mr. Rummage, "but he said he'd return and lead a new march. When he did, though, friends could see he was worried and discouraged. On April 3, he addressed a small rally at the Memphis Mason Temple. That's when he gave his famous 'I've been to the mountain top' speech."

"People still listened to him, then," said Digby.

"Yes, but he felt he'd done all he could. In the speech he said things that made people think he knew something was about to happen to him. He said that although he'd like to live a long time, he wasn't concerned with that now.

He talked about climbing a mountain and seeing the 'promised land.' Then he said he might not get there himself. The next day, on April 4, he was shot and killed by a sniper."

"Oh no," groaned Digby and Hannah.

ASSASSINATION

Dr. King stood on the balcony of his room at the Lorraine Motel in Memphis, Tennessee. It wasn't the room his people had booked. But he'd been asked to use this one by the management, so he did. As he looked on thoughtfully, a shot rang out from the bushes nearby. Dr. King slumped to the floor. A sniper's bullet had found its mark and the most respected civil rights leader in America was dead.

America mourns

At first, no one could believe it. Then the truth of the matter sunk in. Dr. King was gone, and both black and white Americans could only mourn. Some people believed King had been killed because he'd become too popular—and they became very angry. Over the next few days, riots took place in 110 American cities, during which 39 people lost their lives.

Funeral march

April 5 was declared a day of mourning and Dr. King's body was laid in an open coffin at Spelman College in Atlanta so mourners could pay their last respects. His funeral was held at the Ebenezer Baptist Church on April 9. More than 300,000 people marched through Atlanta following the mule-drawn cart that carried his coffin to its final resting place.

A DREAM COME TRUE?

In his famous speech given on the steps of the Lincoln Memorial in 1968, Dr. Martin Luther King, Jr. said:

**"I have a dream...
I have a dream that one day
little black boys and black girls
will be able to join hands with little
white boys and white girls as sisters
and brothers...
I have a dream today."**

A better deal

His dream was the dream of all African Americans who had suffered from racial discrimination, segregation and other injustices that made them second-class citizens in the United States. Dr. King believed he could make that dream come true by peaceful action. His work was responsible for many changes to American law which gave a fairer deal to African Americans.

Inspirational leader

Dr. King's ability to make people listen to him and to inspire them to do something about their situation changed the way African Americans thought about themselves. His words made them feel proud and want to act peacefully for equality. He was a very **charismatic** leader—he had the vision and the personality to attract people to his cause. He showed that the dream could become reality. Because of his influence, many African Americans have risen from poverty to success, and achieved high positions in business, politics, sports, and entertainment.

Hannah held up the microphone as if it was a magic wand. "I'll always treasure this," she said. "I'll remember Dr. King every time I look at it. And I won't use it for any silly stuff."

"Hey," cried Digby, "that's supposed to be mine. I'm the antiques collector."

"Never mind, Digby," said Mr. Clumpmugger, who'd wandered over to Mr. Rummage's stall again, "you can come and read his book of sermons any time you like."

"Yes, but…" began Digby.

"It's all right," interrupted Hannah, "you can have the microphone—as long as I can use it from time to time. I should really hit you over the head with it for being so annoying, but Martin Luther King, Jr's message of non-violent action has stuck in my brain."

"Thank you," said a sheepish-looking Digby. "You can look at it any time you like."

"And you can read Dr. King's sermons too, Hannah," smiled Mr. Clumpmugger.

"I think we've all learned a lot today," said Mr. Rummage as he got up from his seat and stretched. "Well, goodbye for now kids. I hope I'll have something just as interesting for you next week."

"You never let us down," said Digby as he waved goodbye. "And I'll look after this microphone like it was made of gold."

"See ya Mr. Rummage, goodbye Mr. Clumpmugger," said Hannah, who for some reason had forgotten to be quite as disbelieving as she usually was.

MARTIN LUTHER KING JR. DAY

Every year on the third Monday in January, Americans celebrate Martin Luther King, Jr. Day. They celebrate his life and all the great things he did for civil rights. But they also remember what he was fighting for and the injustices that existed during his lifetime.

MARTIN LUTHER KING JR

MAKE IT A DAY ON

NOT A DAY OFF

DAY OF SERVICE

MARTIN LUTHER KING, JR.—A SUCCESS STORY

Who exactly was Martin Luther King, Jr.? Well, he was many people all rolled into one: a minister, a civil rights leader, a social reformer, an author, a thinker, an award winner, and, of course, a parent. He was also a popular speaker who could persuade people to act on things they really believed in. He gave courage to many African Americans.

Dr. King grew up in Atlanta, Georgia, in the southern United States where segregation, racism, and intolerance had been a way of life for generations. Like many people, he knew how wrong all these things were.

He dreamed of a time when the United States would become truly democratic—a country where everyone, regardless of color or religion, would have equal rights. He was to be able to turn a protest into a crusade. That way, a conflict that started locally could be turned into a moral issue the whole nation could be concerned with. He gave hope and inspiration to people everywhere.

Martin Luther King, Jr's, greatest victories were won by appealing to white Americans and putting pressure on the government in Washington. His work didn't die with him. It continues today—and that's why he'll always be remembered.

GLOSSARY

assassination The murder of a famous person

boycott To stop using or buying something or someone to show protest or disapproval

charismatic Describing a leader who excites and motivates people to join his or her cause

civil disobedience Nonviolent refusal to obey certain laws so that governments change them

civil rights A citizen's rights such as free speech, equal legal rights, and freedom from discrimination

democracy A government where all the people have equal power and can vote

integrate To include people from different racial or ethnic groups equally

Ku Klux Klan A secret society organized in the South after the Civil War to make sure that white people had control over black people, in part, through terrorism

lynch To kill someone without legal approval

plantation A large estate or farm on which crops are raised, often by resident workers

racism The belief that race accounts for differences in human character or ability and that a particular race is superior to others

segregation The policy or practice of separating people of different races, classes, or ethnic groups, especially as a form of discrimination

slave A person who is the property of a person or household

INDEX

Other characters in the Stories of Great People series.

KENZO the barber has a wig or hairpiece for every occasion, and is always happy to put his scissors to use!

BUZZ is a street vendor with all the gossip. He sells treats from a tray that's strapped around his neck.

COLONEL KARBUNCLE sells military uniforms, medals, flags, swords, helmets, cannon balls—all from the trunk of his old jeep.

SAFFRON sells pots and pans, herbs, spices, oils, soaps, and dyes from her spice kitchen stall.

Mrs. BILGE pushes her dustcart around the market, picking up litter. Trouble is, she's always throwing away the objects on Mr. Rummage's stall.

CHRISSY's vintage clothing stall has all the costumes Digby and Hannah need to act out the characters in Mr. Rummage's stories.

PRU is a dreamer and Hannah's best friend. She likes to visit the market with Digby and Hannah, especially when makeup and dressing up is involved.

YOUSSEF has traveled to many places around the world. He carries a bag full of souvenirs from his exciting journeys.

JAKE is Digby's friend. He's got a lively imagination and is always up to mischief.

PIXIE the market's fortuneteller sells incense, lotions and potions, candles, mandalas, and crystals inside her exotic stall.

Mr. POLLOCK's toy stall is filled with string puppets, rocking horses, model planes, wooden animals— and he makes them all himself!